The Frog Prince

Hilary Robinson and Jane Abbott

W
FRANKLIN WATTS
LONDON • SYDNEY

1
The Golden Ball

Long, long ago, in a castle by a wood, lived
a beautiful princess. She spent her days
dancing in the gardens and playing with
her magical golden ball. The ball had been
a gift from her godmother who said that it
would always bring the princess great
happiness, but that she must always look
after it.

On summer days, the princess loved to skip down the woodland path by the castle. Deep in the wood was a wishing well.

She enjoyed playing with the frogs, birds and minibeasts, and she liked to collect wild flowers. The princess always took her magical golden ball with her, bouncing and catching it as she ran.

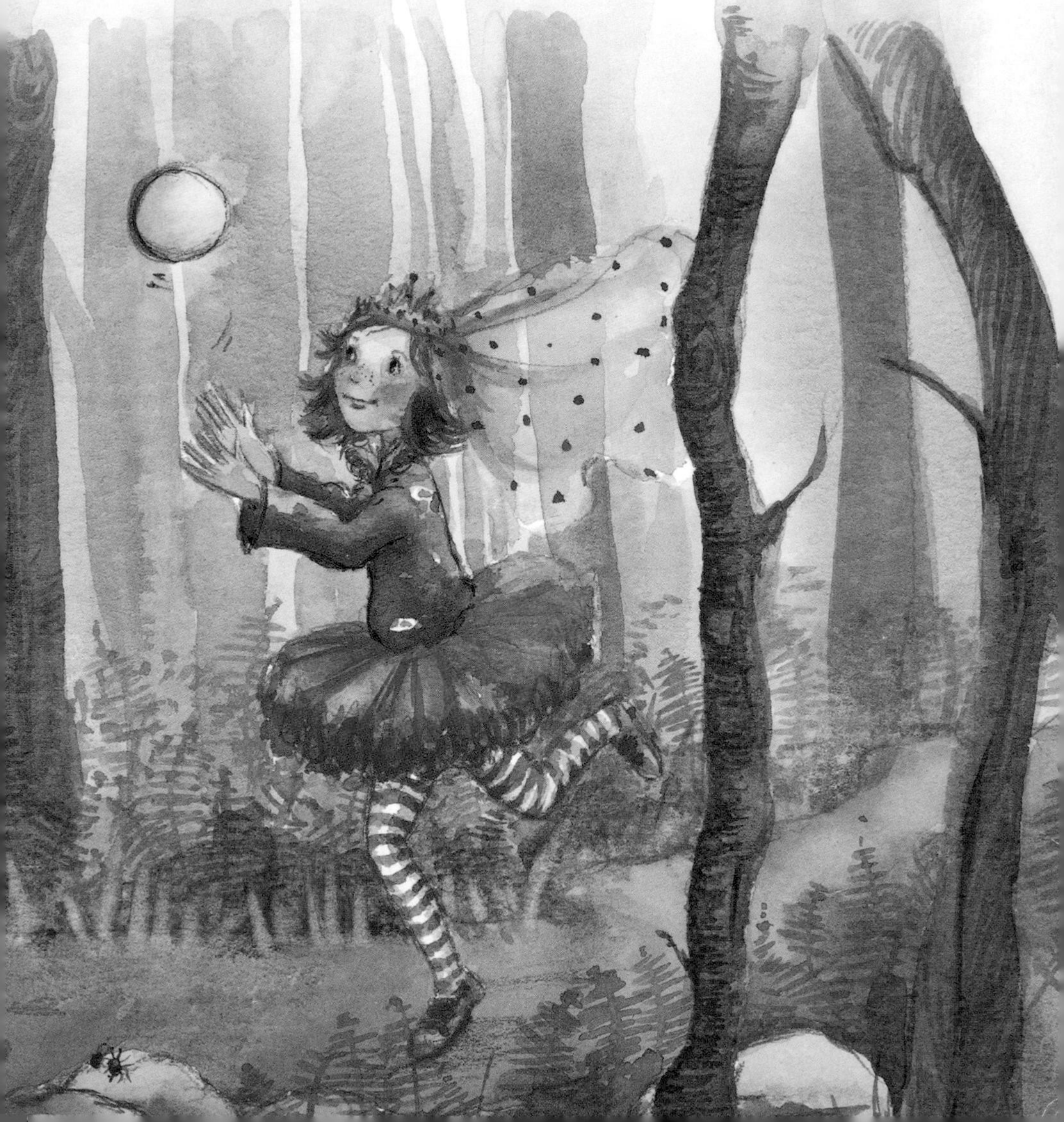

"I wonder what the birds will do if I throw my golden ball very high," she thought to herself. "One, two, three!" she yelled, and she threw the ball as high as she could. The birds flapped their wings and then, disaster!

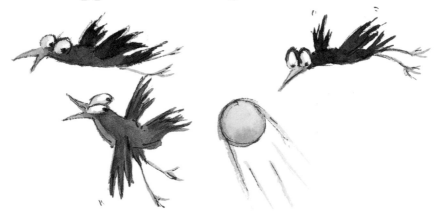

The golden ball dropped into the well with a loud splash.

"On no!" cried the princess. "I've lost my
golden ball. Whatever will my godmother
say?" She sat on the edge of the well
and wept.

2
A Friendly Frog

As she wept, a kindly frog leapt up and
sat beside her. "Why are you weeping?"
he asked. "Is it because you have lost your
golden ball? I saw you playing and I saw it
drop into the well."

"Yes," said the princess, tearfully. "It was a
gift from my godmother and she will never,
ever forgive me for being so
careless with such a
precious gift."

The frog thought for a few moments.

"If I dive into the well and find your golden ball will you promise to be my friend?" he asked. "Will you promise to be my friend for ever and ever?"

"I promise I will always be your friend if you find my golden ball!" said the princess.

"My godmother said it would bring me great happiness and perhaps, just perhaps, it will bring us both great happiness!"

"Wait here," said the frog. He jumped into the wishing well. A short while later, he scrambled out, clutching the ball. He sat on the edge of the well and handed the ball back to the princess. She was overjoyed! "Thank you so much!" she said.

Then, forgetting her promise, she jumped
up, turned away and ran back towards the
castle, bouncing and catching the ball as she
ran. The frog looked puzzled. He had a plan.
"If that golden ball is to bring us both
happiness," he said to himself, "then I need
to try and get the princess to lay her hand
on me first."

3

A Promise is a Promise

The next day, the frog hopped all the way up the woodland path and rattled the knocker on the castle door. The princess was having breakfast with her parents.

"Princess, Princess, please let me in,"
croaked a voice. "Please show me some
mercy and answer the door. I need to
speak to you. You promised you would
be my friend."

The princess opened the door and looked
out. "You're not welcome here!" she said.
"Go back to the wishing well where you
belong. Go back to your woodland friends,
to the birds, the rabbits and the minibeasts."

Then she slammed the door. The frog
stayed where he was and listened.

Back at the table, the princess sat down and carried on eating without saying a word. "Who was that?" asked the king. "Who came to the door and asked for you?"

"It was just an ugly frog," replied the
princess. "I promised him I would always be
his friend if he found my golden ball for me.
I was careless and let it drop in the well. The
frog dived in and got it back for me."

"You promised the frog you would always be his friend if he found your ball?" asked the king. "You made a promise?"

"Yes, I did," said the princess.

"Well then, you must be his friend," said the king. "Invite him in. A promise is a promise, and promises must be kept," he added sternly.

So the frog came in and sat beside the princess. The princess was not happy that the frog was helping himself to cereal from her bowl. He touched her shoulder, hoping she would hold his hand. But she didn't.

4
A Princess's Touch

Later that day, while the royal family were having dinner, the frog jumped onto the table and ate from the princess's plate. He was hoping that she would push him away. She didn't. The king would not have approved so she just ignored him.

Then, at bedtime, the frog jumped onto her bed.

"No!" shouted the princess. "Go away! Go back to the wishing well. Go and play with your woodland friends. The castle is not the place for a frog." And with that she pushed the frog away just as he had hoped!

For only then could he turn into...

a handsome prince! The princess looked on
in shock. "You're not really a frog, are you?"
she said. "You're a prince. Who turned you
into a frog?"

The prince told her that many years ago
a wicked witch had taken revenge on his
family and turned him into a frog. The
witch said that only the touch of a princess's
hand could save him and return
him to his former self. Then
the witch banished him to
live in a well, believing
he would never be
found by a princess.

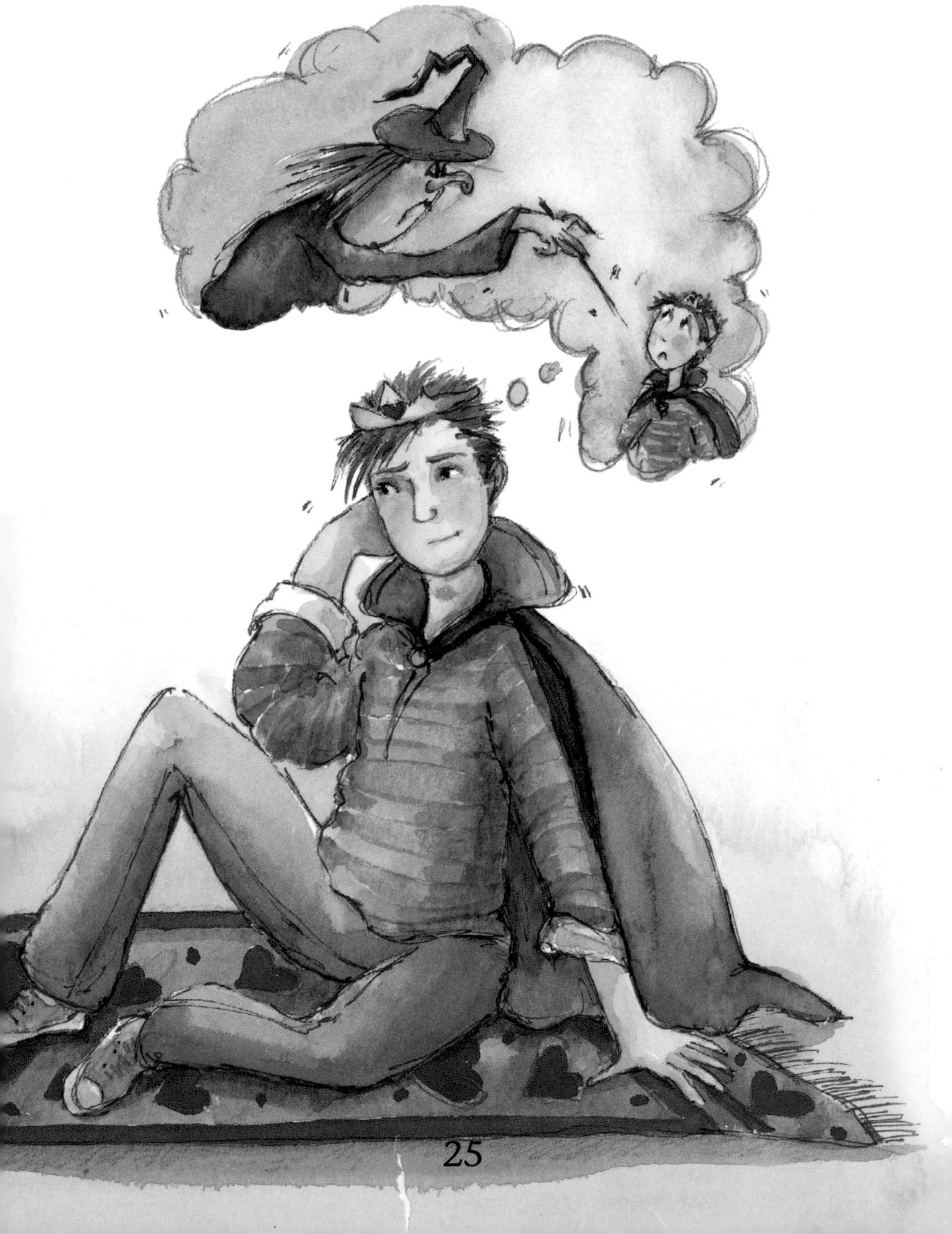

5
The Happy Couple

A few days later, while the princess was out walking in the woods, she bumped into the prince again.

"You have saved me from a lifetime of living as a frog," said the prince. "And I think your golden ball has brought us together for a reason. I stayed nearby as I have to ask: Will you marry me?"

The princess happily agreed. So the prince and the princess were soon married, and they were showered with flowers from the woodland where they had met.

The golden ball had indeed brought the princess great happiness, just as her godmother had promised.

About the story

The Frog Prince is a European fairy tale. The Brothers Grimm included a version of the tale in their collection of stories in 1812. In modern versions of the tale, the princess must kiss the frog for him to transform into a prince. However, in the original Grimm version the frog is transformed when the princess throws the frog against the wall in disgust.

The fairy tale has given rise to the popular phrase: "You must kiss a lot of frogs before you meet your prince." The story has featured in popular music and in a children's opera. It was also used as the basis for the Disney film *The Princess and the Frog.*

Be in the story!

Imagine you are
the prince and you
have just transformed
from being a frog.
How do you feel about
the princess?

Now imagine you are
the princess. How do
you feel about your
behaviour towards
the frog now that he
has changed into a
prince?

Franklin Watts
First published in Great Britain in 2016 by The Watts Publishing Group

Copyright (text) © Hilary Robinson 2016
Copyright (illustrations) © Jane Abbott 2005

Series Editor: Jackie Hamley
Series Advisor: Catherine Glavina
Series Designer: Cathryn Gilbert

A CIP catalogue record for this book is available
from the British Library.

The artwork for this story first appeared in
Leapfrog Fairy Tales: The Frog Prince

ISBN 978 1 4451 4665 2 (hbk)
ISBN 978 1 4451 4666 9 (library ebook)
ISBN 978 1 4451 4667 6 (pbk)

Printed in China

Franklin Watts
An imprint of
Hachette Children's Group
Part of The Watts Publishing Group
Carmelite House
50 Victoria Embankment
London EC4Y 0DZ

An Hachette UK Company
www.hachette.co.uk

www.franklinwatts.co.uk

FSC
www.fsc.org
MIX
Paper from
responsible sources
FSC® C104740